Ellie Ultra is published by Stone Arch Books,
A Capstone Imprint
1710 Roe Crest Drive
North Mankato, Minnesota 56003
www.mycapstone.com

For Milla, who makes my heart double in size—love, Mom

Library of Congress Cataloging-in-Publication Data is
available on the Library of Congress website.

ISBN: 978-1-4965-6513-6 (hardcover)
ISBN: 978-1-4965-6517-4 (paperback)
ISBN: 978-1-4965-6515-0 (eBook PDF)

Summary: Ellie can't wait to go to Camp Hero! But when
her cabinmates, superhero twins Mona and Leona, give
her the cold shoulder, Ellie decides to use her parents'
latest invention to get them to like her. The invention
works too well, and the twins start fighting over Ellie!
Can Ellie stop their double trouble and find out why they
weren't friendly to her in the first place?

Designer: Tracy McCabe

Printed in the United States of America.
PA017

Camp Hero
Double Trouble

written by Gina Bellisario

illustrated by Jessika von Innerebner

STONE ARCH BOOKS
a capstone imprint

TABLE OF CONTENTS

CHAPTER 1

Camp Hero

It was just another day in the city of Winkopolis. Swimmers swam. Hikers hiked. Crafters crafted. Everyone was doing the same old ordinary things. Everyone, mind you, but the girl who lived at 8 Louise Lane.

That girl was Ellie Ultra. She was flipping through her camper's guide, quicker than a dolphin with a turbo-charged tail. It was *extra*ordinary.

At the kitchen table, Ellie scanned the pages excitedly. There were pictures of kids climbing, splashing, and swinging. All of them wore superhero capes.

"Camp Hero starts tomorrow!" Ellie told her best friend, Hannah. "I'm going for a whole week. Isn't that awesome?"

"You're so lucky," Hannah said. "I had a great time when I went last spring break. Did you see the activity schedule?" She pointed to a sheet of paper sticking out of the guide.

Ellie pulled out the schedule and started reading. Her forehead crinkled. None of the activities involved saving the world. It seemed strange for a place called Camp *Hero*. After all, as a superhero, coming to the rescue was what Ellie did best.

"Um, Hannah? Isn't the camp for heroes?" Ellie asked. "There's nothing about fighting villains on here. Will I get to crush a doomsday device, at least?"

Hannah giggled. "Not exactly," she replied. "But you'll still do super stuff. There's Mega Splash Hour and High-Flying Trampoline Dodgeball. And check out the Boom! Pow! Obstacle Course. . . ." She pointed to a picture at the bottom of the paper.

Looking closely, Ellie saw campers jumping into foam blocks. *It's probably nicer than jumping into toxic ooze,* she thought. She'd been forced to do that while chasing a mad scientist. Getting the ooze off her shoes had taken *forever.*

"There's also the Super Friend Campfire," Hannah continued. "It's at the end of the week. You eat marshmallows and play games. And you do the official Camp Hero cheer."

"How does the cheer go?" Ellie asked.

Hannah cleared her throat. Then she sang:

> Let's hear it for the camp
> where the action never ends!
> Camp Hero, Camp Hero,
> the place for super friends!

Ellie's excitement faded a little. *Her* super friend wouldn't be at camp. Hannah had to stay home this year so she could watch her kid sister, Cece, while their mom worked from home.

"I wish you could come to camp with me," Ellie said.

"Me too," Hannah replied. "But you'll do a lot with your cabinmates. You'll learn about them at the first activity." She pointed to the top of the schedule. "It's called Meet the Hero. Don't forget to bring something with you to share. It should be special."

What should I share? Ellie wondered. It couldn't be just anything. This would be her chance to make a good first impression.

Suddenly—*Ka-Zap!*—an idea electrified her brainpower.

"I know! I can share my Princess Power ring," Ellie said. "It came with the first-ever Princess Power comic book. It changes color with your mood. It turns blue for calm, yellow for happy, and pink for powerful." She flew out of her seat. "Let me show you."

Just then Ellie's best dog friend, Super Fluffy, bounded over, tail wagging. He held the ring in his mouth. It was yellow.

With a sigh, Ellie crossed her arms. Her dog had a bad habit of swiping her stuff. Sometimes, he was worse than the worst thief in Winkopolis.

"Oh, Fluffster! Give that back."

Super Fluffy crouched low, ready to play, as Ellie reached for the ring. He took off across the floor, but his fast feet were no match for his owner's quick thinking. Turning invisible, she roared ahead of her pup and circled into his path. Super Fluffy ran straight into her arms.

That trick works every time, Ellie thought, reappearing with a smile.

Super Fluffy let out a whimper, his mouth now empty.

"Where did my ring go?" Blinking on her X-ray vision, Ellie scanned the floor with her eye beams. But she only saw crumbs from breakfast.

Ellie got a sinking feeling. *I'd better check one more place,* she thought.

Her beams traveled over Super Fluffy's belly. Sure enough, the ring was inside. It sat between a crayon and a half-chewed eraser.

"I guess I'll have to share something else for Meet the Hero," Ellie said. She lifted a scolding eyebrow at her pup, and his ears flattened. "I'll take care of you later. Until then, paws off my things, OK?"

With a whine, Super Fluffy disappeared up the stairs. Ellie shook her head, then closed her guide.

"I should finish packing," she told Hannah. "I still need to fit my rain boots, sunblock, swimsuit, and Ice Boy comic books into my bag. When I'm done, my suitcase will be heavier than a robo-bear!"

"I'll miss you," Hannah said as they walked to the door. "Hey! Why don't you write me? I'll write you back."

Ellie smiled. "I'll do that."

Before skipping out, Hannah paused. "I almost forgot! You need to know the hero handshake. It's the camp greeting."

Hannah did the movements, and Ellie followed along. First they bumped fists. Then they punched the sky. Finally they stuck their hands on their hips, threw their shoulders back, and flashed winning grins.

Ellie grinned extra wide. She struck the same pose whenever she stopped a super-villain. "Camp Hero, here I come!"

CHAPTER 2

The Ultra Hypno Change-O

After Hannah left, Ellie packed the rest of her supplies. Fitting everything into her suitcase seemed impossible at first. But her muscle power handled the job, no sweat. She had just found her stationery when Mom walked into the room.

"Whoa, your suitcase is stuffed," Mom said, eyeing the bulging bag. "Have you finished packing? I'm not sure you can squeeze in anything else, even with your super strength."

"I need one last thing," Ellie said. "I have to talk about an item at the first activity, Meet the Hero. It *was* going to be my Princess Power ring. That is, until Super Fluffy ate it." She made a face. "I guess it will come out . . . eventually. . . ."

Super Fluffy was sitting on Ellie's bed. He quietly got up and slipped under her blanket. Her words had clearly embarrassed him.

"Let's find something else for you," Mom said, glancing around. Her eyes stopped at a certificate on the bulletin board. "What about your Hero Student Award? I remember when you got it for saving your classmates."

"It *is* a good idea," Ellie admitted. "But I'm not sure it's what I want. What if the other kids bring their awards? I need an item that will stand out."

"What about your Most Helpful Citizen ribbon?" Mom suggested. She pointed to a blue ribbon pinned next to Ellie's certificate. It had been a gift from the mayor after Ellie rescued him from being eaten by a giant mutant meatball.

"I'm not sure about that either," Ellie replied. "Kids will probably bring their ribbons too."

Just then Mom saw Ellie's cape in the mirror. "I've got it!" She clapped her hands. "You can share your cape. It's pretty heroic, don't you think?"

Ellie smiled at the pink cloth. It was her most special belonging. But Hannah had mentioned that lots of campers wore capes for fun. Hers would hardly be unique.

Turning away from her reflection, she replied, "Maybe I can share something different from my usual superhero stuff? That stuff is super,

but I want something *extra* special." Suddenly
a thought came to her. "And I know where to
find it!"

Mom followed as Ellie flew downstairs to
the laboratory. Ellie's parents were super-genius
scientists who created the inventions for B.R.A.I.N.,
a group that protected the city against villains.

Their lab was filled with special tools like
night-vision goggles and anti-gravity sneakers.
Mom and Dad used the tools to build extra-special
inventions.

Ellie floated toward the entrance to the Gadget
Gallery. The gallery stored Mom and Dad's
creations.

"Can I bring an invention?" she asked. "All
the campers are going to share something about
themselves. I want to talk about my superhero
family instead. It makes me proud."

Mom's face brightened. "How lovely! I think that would be all right. I'm sure Dad and B.R.A.I.N. wouldn't mind, either." She put her arm around Ellie and led her into the room. "Let's pick out a gadget for you."

Ellie puzzled over her choices as they headed for the wall of inventions. Should she take the Ultra Slippy Grippy? It stopped the evil Sticky Fingers, who took everything from basketballs to drumsticks. Or maybe the Ultra Cheer-Me-Up? It sweetened the sour mood of Ho Ho Hum. Every Christmas, that villain visited Winkopolis to spread holiday gloom.

She was deep in thought when her super ears picked up a shuffling noise. Suddenly a voice cried out: "Help!"

Nothing could get a superhero's attention like someone in need of rescuing! Ellie turned to see Dad at the far end of the gallery, lifting a heavy

invention off the wall. Its weight was overpowering him. His arms were shaking. His knees were buckling.

Fast as a flash, Ellie ran to his side and scooped up the invention. Then she placed it on a nearby cart, which already held the Ultra Time Traveler, the Ultra Repeat Repeat, and other gadgets.

Dad wiped his brow in relief. "Thanks for the hand," he told Ellie. "I'm taking down our old inventions. But some of them are heavier than I thought."

"Are you bringing them to B.R.A.I.N. headquarters?" Ellie asked. "I wanted one to talk about at Camp Hero."

"I'm just making space for new ones," Dad said. "But I put some in that closet." He motioned to a door on the back wall. "We agreed to hold on to a few, just in case. We can use them to protect the lab if a villain shows up to steal something. Having some extra power around here will come in handy!"

Ellie zipped over and opened the door. Cyclops, the Ultras' giant, one-eyed iguana, sat on a shelf inside. "Hey, Cyclops!" she said.

The iguana greeted Ellie with a kind wave. Then he went back to placing inventions into cubbies. He had labeled them with the letters A to Z.

"Wow, Cy," Ellie said, marveling at his skills. "You're good at closet organizing. I know it's just your new hobby, but you could start a business!"

Cyclops took a small card out of his tool belt. It read:

Is your closet messy?

Call 1-800-CYCLOPS

The lizard that's green . . . and clean!

Maybe I should call Cyclops, Ellie thought. *My closet is a mighty mess.*

As Cyclops got back to work, Ellie X-rayed the cubbies, looking for an invention. Her eye beams moved left to right, revealing gadget after gadget. Some of them had large wheels. Others had tubes sticking out in every direction.

Mom poked her head in the doorway. "Have you found something?" she asked.

"Nah," Ellie replied. Her beams blinked off. "These inventions are too big. They would never fit in my suitcase."

Reaching over Ellie's shoulder, Mom opened the cubby that was marked with an H. She dug around inside, then pulled out a round invention. It fit in the palm of her hand.

"This one is pocket-sized," she said. "It's our latest invention, the Ultra Hypno Change-O."

Mom turned a dial on the back. Black and white lines appeared on the face of the gadget. They swirled in a mesmerizing circle.

"I know what this invention does!" Ellie said. "It hypnotizes people, right? Does it make them act silly? Or crow like a rooster?" She threw her head back and cock-a-doodle-doed.

"It *does* hypnotize people," Mom replied. "But it only makes them behave in the opposite way. For example, if they were acting stubborn, it would make them cooperative. If they were acting rude, it would make them polite. The effect can also be reversed." She turned the dial the other way, and the lines went backward.

Mom shut off the Ultra Hypno Change-O, then handed it to Ellie. "I trust you'll share this gadget safely," she said. "It's powerful, and that's nothing to play with. Sometimes power can do more harm than good."

Ellie understood. Not long ago, she'd made a clone of herself using the Ultra Copy Button. She'd only wanted her copy to help water flowers for a school project. But instead, it had gone overboard and almost flooded the planet.

"I'll be safe," she promised. "Cross my cape!"

Taking off, Ellie went to pack the gadget. She couldn't wait to show it to her cabinmates. It was sure to be the start of a super friendship.

CHAPTER 3

A Frosty Hello

"Off to Camp Hero!" Dad said in the car on Monday morning. He turned to Ellie as Mom buckled up. "Are you ready, Ellie?"

"Yes!" Ellie squealed in the back seat. "Camp is going to be so fun. Even more fun than busting an alien blob!"

As they drove away, Ellie looked out the window. She watched as Winkopolis got smaller until the city disappeared.

"Bye, Hannah," she whispered. "I'll write soon!"

For the next hour, they cruised along the highway. Ellie passed the time playing cards by herself. She breezed through twenty games of Memory before they finally arrived at the campground.

Ellie peered out the window. Camp Hero looked even better than it had in the guide! On one side, a lake glistened. It had a dock with inner tubes, rafts, and paddleboats. On the other side, there was a court with games like four square and hopscotch.

Cabins sat in the center of the grounds. They were gathered around an open clearing, where campers hung out on log benches. Some greeted each other with the hero handshake. A couple of kids waved to Ellie as the car went past.

Those campers are friendly, she thought. *Maybe they're my cabinmates!*

After parking they went to the visitors' center. Ellie was waiting with her parents to check in when a young woman wearing a cape walked up.

"Ellie Ultra! I've been expecting you," she said cheerfully. She pointed to Ellie's name on a clipboard.

"How did you know it was me? Can you read my mind?" Ellie asked. "I have that power, but it only works on people. *Not* robot minions, unfortunately . . ."

"I heard you're a real superhero. That's amazing!" the woman replied. "As for me? I read your name on the back of your cape. My name is on my cape too." She turned and pointed.

"Wendy the Whiz," Ellie said, scanning the words. "I like it! It sounds very hero-y."

"Thanks! You can also call me Wendy," she replied with a wink. "I'm your camp counselor, so I'll lead your activities this week." She picked up Ellie's bag. "Let's meet your cabinmates. They're real superheroes like you!"

Real superheroes? Ellie couldn't believe her supersonic hearing. They were going to have a blast together! They could race a jet and surf a tidal wave. They could even save a town or two!

Ellie flew into Mom and Dad's arms. "Remember to play fetch with Super Fluffy," she said, hugging them, "and don't forget to read to Cyclops at bedtime. His favorite book is *The Little Lizard That Could*."

"Everything will be in good hands," Mom reassured her.

After saying goodbye, Ellie followed Wendy toward the campers' quarters. They went down a trail speckled with fallen acorns. As they passed under a shady oak, one almost fell on Ellie's noggin. Ellie glanced up, worried a squirrel minion was up to trouble, but luckily, she only saw a plain old squirrel.

"Here we are!" Wendy announced when they reached the cabins. Each one was labeled with a name, like *High Fliers* or *Smart Squad*. Wendy stepped up to a cabin labeled *Kid Wonders* and unlocked the door.

As Ellie flew in, a burst of icy air hit her. *Brrr!* she thought with a shiver. The room felt like Antarctica on an extra-cold day. Where was the chill coming from?

Ellie glanced around the room. Nothing seemed out of the ordinary. Beds with storage cabinets lined the wall. Two of them had been claimed. The beds had matching blankets with penguin patterns.

Just then a remarkable sight caught Ellie's eye. In the corner stood a smiling snowman. It had twigs for arms, rocks for eyes and a mouth, and a pine cone for a nose. Two girls were skipping around the frosty creation, giggling and tossing snow at each other. Snowflakes swirled out of their hands in a crystal mist.

Extraordinary! Ellie thought. She had only seen her parents make snow before. But Mom and Dad needed the help of the Ultra Weather Machine to do it.

Catching sight of Ellie, the girls stopped playing. They exchanged unsure glances.

"This is Mona and Leona Winter," Wendy said, introducing them.

"I'm Mona—" said the one girl.

"—and I'm Leona," said the other girl.

"We're twins," they said together.

Standing side-by-side, Mona and Leona looked strikingly similar. They were the same height, and their hair was identical. They also had the same number of freckles, according to Ellie's lightning-quick calculations. Only their outfits were slightly different: Mona wore leggings, while Leona had on shorts and knee socks.

"Hi! I'm Ellie," Ellie replied. "You can freeze stuff, huh? That's cool! I can melt things—it's one of my powers. See?" She made her fists flare up, then put out the fire. "Anyway, want to do the hero handshake?"

Ellie's hand was still smoking when she held it out to the twins. They shook their heads and took a cautious step back.

"I'm sure you'll all get along," Wendy said as Ellie quickly blew out the smoke. "Maybe Mona and Leona can help you unpack. But don't take long! It's almost time for Meet the Hero."

She checked her watch. "In fact, come to the clearing when you're finished. And bring the item you're sharing, OK?" She set Ellie's suitcase on an empty bed before leaving.

Mona pulled at Leona's elbow, then stepped toward the door. Ellie raced past the girls to her bag. She couldn't wait to show off the Ultra Hypno Change-O. It was going to dazzle them!

"Check out what I brought!" she said, digging out the gadget. "It belongs to my parents. They fight villains like we do." She swung around and smiled. But the only thing smiling back was the snowman.

Suddenly the cabin door banged shut. Peeking out the screen, Ellie saw Mona and Leona. A frozen path formed under their feet as they glided to the clearing, arms linked.

They left for the activity? Without me? Ellie was confused. She thought her cabinmates would be friendlier. But they seemed cold, even for superheroes with freezing power.

* * *

After getting herself settled, Ellie skipped off to Meet the Hero. Mona and Leona probably just needed time to get to know her. Then they would warm up, no doubt.

The benches were crowded when she flew into the clearing. Ellie hoped the girls had saved her a seat, but a boy was sitting next to Mona. Leona was on her sister's other side at the end of the bench. They were playing tic-tac-toe, using icicles to draw in the gravel.

"Here's a spot, Ellie!" Wendy called from another log. She patted the space next to her, and Ellie went quietly to sit down.

Wendy raised her clipboard to get everyone's attention. "Welcome, heroes!" she said. "For this activity, we're all going to share something special. Let's go around, and you can tell us what makes your item so super." She pointed to Leona. "Leona? Would you like to start?"

Leona paused and looked at Mona. Then she looked back at Wendy. "Can I take my turn with Mona?" she asked.

"We have the same items," Mona added.

Wendy nodded, and the girls took out identical gold medals. They had pictures of ice skates on the front.

"We won these medals—" Mona began.

"—for pair figure skating," Leona went on.

"The competition was tough—"

"—so we were nervous."

"After we did a loop jump—"

"—we spun around too fast—"

"—and made a blizzard on the ice rink."

"It was kind of embarrassing," both girls said. "But we got first place!"

Ellie watched as they high-fived, clinking their medals. They clearly had a close friendship—so close they even finished each other's sentences.

Maybe they'll make room for one more friend, she thought hopefully.

The circle of sharing continued. Campers talked about a trophy from a horse show, a volunteer badge, and a handmade ornament.

Finally it was Ellie's turn. She pulled the Ultra Hypno Change-O out of her pocket. "My parents made this invention," she said. "It's very special."

Leona was drawing a snowy owl on the ground. Mona nudged her and pointed to the Hypno Change-O. They stared curiously.

"They build inventions that help save the world," Ellie said. She turned on the gadget, and the mesmerizing lines appeared. "See these lines? They can change someone's behavior from bad to good. That's how it helps stop villains. They never behave!"

A few campers leaned forward for a better look. Right away, Ellie shut off the Ultra Hypno Change-O. She didn't want it taking effect.

"Wow, heroes! Your items are all very special, indeed," Wendy said. She stood up in front of the group. "Our activity is over, but have no fear! This week you'll have more fun with your cabinmates. I know you'll become friends, and at the end of camp, you can celebrate your new friendships at the Super Friend Campfire!" She dismissed everyone for the next activity, Mega Splash Hour.

Mona and Leona jumped to their feet. They held hands and squealed.

"We're going to have the best time—"

"—at the Super Friend Campfire!"

They glided past Ellie, and an icy breeze rolled off their backs. It made Ellie shiver. If Mona and Leona didn't warm up to her, how could she become their friend?

CHAPTER 4

Iced Out

Everyone scattered to get ready for Mega Splash Hour—sixty minutes of free time at the lake. Campers could swim, float on colorful inner tubes and water noodles, and go paddle-boating.

Ellie put her swimsuit and towel into her beach bag. *I know I can have fun with Mona and Leona,* she thought. *I'll show them my super skills. Then they'll see all the things I can do!*

Down by the dock, kids were splashing around. Ellie flew toward the changing stalls when suddenly her ears picked up a crackling noise. It sounded like water freezing over.

She followed the noise to the end of the beach. Mona and Leona were standing at the shoreline, using their powers to make an ice rink. A crystal mist sprayed out of their hands and fell over a quiet part of the lake, turning the water solid.

Once the top was frozen, the girls skipped onto the ice with ease. Fish swam beneath the surface.

"Excuse me, Mona and Leona?" Ellie asked, sailing over to them. "I don't mean to interrupt, but . . . do you want to play? I was about to change into my swimsuit."

Mona crossed her arms. "Well—" she began.

"—we're not swimming," Leona continued.

"Instead—"

"No—"

"—thanks."

"How about we play water volleyball?" Ellie suggested. "Or take a raft ride? Or go snorkeling? I'll do whatever—your choice!"

The girls stayed quiet. Mona tugged at her shirt. Leona picked at her thumbnail.

Ellie could tell they wanted to do something, but what? *I'll read their minds and find out,* she thought. *Then we can start having fun.*

Her brainpower buzzing like a TV antenna, Ellie tuned into the twins' thoughts. She saw images of them cannonballing into the water and playing volleyball. She saw Mona pushing Leona on a raft, pretending to be the engine on a motorboat.

Ellie deflated. There was one big problem—she hadn't seen herself in any of the images.

"I think I'll go snorkeling," she said, retreating into her own thoughts. She'd felt a brain freeze coming on. "Maybe I'll see you soon?"

The twins didn't hesitate or reply before skating off. Ellie sighed and grabbed her beach bag. Maybe the fish were in a friendlier mood.

CHAPTER 5

Help, Hannah!

When Mega Splash Hour ended, Ellie ate
a lonely lunch. An ant offered a little company.
It snacked on a corn chip that had fallen off
her tray.

"I wish you were the comic book superhero,
Astro Ant," she said to the bug. "We could hang
out and play asteroid baseball."

Just then Wendy came into the dining hall.
"High-Flying Trampoline Dodgeball starts in ten

minutes!" she announced. "Meet me at the rec center, and get ready to soar, heroes!" Her cape flapped behind her as she skipped out.

In a flash, everyone jumped up from their seats. Kids quickly piled their dirty dishes in the sink. Then they left for the activity, ignoring the trash still sitting on the tables.

Ellie frowned. "Heroes should have better manners," she said.

Her pick-up trick would take care of the litter. Spinning into a vortex, she pulled in crumpled napkins and mayonnaise packets. She stopped over a wastebasket to let everything drop in, then hurried to the rec center.

The place was hopping when Ellie arrived. Campers bounced on a trampoline court. Wendy was splitting everyone into teams and passing out dodgeballs.

"Guess I'll have to sit this game out," Ellie said as Wendy gave away the last ball. She turned toward the bench when she spotted Mona waving in her direction.

Mona held up a dodgeball. "I got one for you!" she called.

"For me?" Ellie's heart leaped like a turbo-powered toad. Maybe she was wrong about her cabinmates. Maybe they really *were* friendly!

With a springy step, Ellie went to join Mona. But before she'd gone far, Leona glided past her from the drinking fountain.

"Thanks!" Leona said, sliding up to her sister. She took the ball, and they jumped onto the court.

Mona wasn't being nice to me after all, Ellie realized. Disappointed, she blinked herself invisible and left the rec center. She didn't feel much like playing anymore.

Ellie skipped activities for the rest of the day. Instead, she curled up with her comic books. She spent most of her time with Princess Power and the princess' sidekick, Steel Blossom.

If only I had my own super friend, Ellie thought as Steel Blossom helped battle the evil Troll King. *At least then I would have company at the campfire on Friday. I wish Hannah were here. . . .*

That gave her an idea! Ellie put her comic down, then took out her stationery, and wrote:

Dear Hannah,

I MISS YOU! Camp isn't going very well. My cabinmates are cold—literally! They're superheroes who can freeze stuff, but they're acting frosty to me too. They only hang out with each other and pretend I'm invisible. Even when I'm not using my powers!

How can I be their friend? If I have to spend the whole week alone, I'm DOOMED.

YSB (Your Super Bestie),

Ellie

P.S. Write back soon!

Ellie stuffed the letter into an envelope. As she dug through her suitcase for a stamp, the Ultra Hypno Change-O fell out.

I could use the Hypno Change-O on Mona and Leona, she thought, eyeing the gadget. *Then they would be friendly to me.*

It would be a nice change. She'd have to keep her promise to Mom and be careful. But how could anything go wrong? The gadget was invented to do good. It wouldn't make anyone behave badly.

Her spirits lifting, Ellie dropped Hannah's letter into the mailbox. It wouldn't be long before she made a camp friend—times two!

CHAPTER 6

Hot and Cold

On Tuesday, Ellie waited for her cabinmates to get ready for the first activity. In her hand, the Ultra Hypno Change-O hummed with mesmerizing might.

Soon Leona came out of the bathroom. She was brushing frost out of her hair. Mona followed, spinning a snowball on her finger.

Mona froze as Ellie held out the Hypno Change-O. It seemed to fascinate her. She tapped Leona, alerting her to the gadget.

"Isn't that what you shared—"

"—at Meet the Hero?"

Ellie nodded as the girls approached. "I saw you looking at it," she said. "If you want, I can give you a *closer* look."

As Leona peeked over Mona's shoulder, Ellie turned the gadget's dial. The black and white lines appeared, capturing the twins' attention. The lines spun in rhythmic circles and pulled them into a deep, mind-bending sleep. Their faces went blank. Seconds later, smiles as warm as mittens spread across their cheeks.

"Ellie, you have—"

"—the most awesome stuff!"

"We love your shirt, your shoes—"

"—and your cape!"

"Let's get the day started—"

"—so we can have fun!"

Mona picked up Ellie's towel. Leona hurried to grab Ellie's beach bag.

Ellie watched in amazement. *Mom wasn't kidding*, she thought. *The Hypno Change-O is strong!* It had melted away her cabinmates' icy behavior.

With Ellie in the middle, the trio went to the lake for Mega Splash Hour. They passed Wendy, who was stacking inner tubes on the dock.

"Wow!" Wendy exclaimed. "The three of you are really getting along. I knew you would."

Ellie smiled weakly. So what if that wasn't exactly the truth? At least the twins were being kind to her.

As they came up to the equipment, Ellie wondered if the girls would consider something besides speed skating. Her bottom had a way-bad bruise from yesterday's attempt.

"Do you want to play a game?" Ellie asked. "Ring toss with the water noodles? Inner tube races?"

"Sure, we can—"

"—do that."

"Or, if you'd like, we can take a paddleboat ride," Ellie said. "I can give us a super-powered push onto the water."

"Of course—"

"—count us in!"

Ellie scrunched her eyebrows. They were agreeing to do whatever she suggested. It must be the Hypno Change-O talking. "I guess we'll go on a ride. . . ."

The paddleboats were lined up neatly. Ellie went to pluck one from the row, but as she got closer, she realized something. The boats only had two seats.

"Can I go—"

"—with you, Ellie?"

Clasping their hands, both girls waited hopefully for Ellie's answer.

"Hmm . . ." Ellie bit her lip as she glanced between them. It didn't seem right to choose one sister over the other. "Maybe you can play Rock-Paper-Scissors, and I'll go with the winner?" she offered. "I always play that game with my pet iguana. It's how we pick who goes first in dominoes."

The pair faced off. "I won!" Mona cheered after her paper beat Leona's rock. She put on a life jacket and climbed into her seat. "C'mon, Ellie! Let's go!"

"Right behind you," Ellie said, giggling. It tickled her to be treated so well. She flew over to launch the craft when she heard someone sigh. The sound stopped her in midair. Leona, looking sullen, was walking off to the side.

"No fair," Leona muttered. "Mona gets to go with Ellie, and I'm stuck here." She slumped down onto the dock.

Leona sounds mad at Mona, Ellie thought. *Next time I'll try to include both of them. That way, no one feels left out.* She didn't want to cause any hard feelings, especially between friends.

* * *

At lunch Ellie made sure they all sat together. Her X-ray beams shined through the crowd, locating three empty seats in the corner. She sat down, and the girls flanked her sides like bread on a hero sandwich.

The food was good. But the company was better. Mona kept Ellie's water glass filled, and Leona glided over to the silverware to grab a spoon for Ellie's soup. Leona also got more crackers when Ellie ran out.

As Ellie crumbled a cracker into her bowl, something extra crunchy rolled by on the dessert cart. "Ooo, rice crispy treats!" she said. The cart was carrying enough treats for every camper in the hall. "Those are my favorite."

"Your favorite?" the girls repeated, perking up.

"We'll save them—"

"—for you!"

Frozen mist sprayed out of the twins' fingers. It hit the platter, encasing the treats in a block of ice.

Ellie's face got hot as the other campers glared at their table. They looked at her like she was the dessert-snatching Cookie Crook.

"How, um . . . thoughtful!" she said to the girls. "It's nice of you to offer. But one treat is plenty for me." She put her hands on the ice-block, melting it with her super-heating power. The treats were soggy, but after another burst of heat, they were crispier than ever.

After eating, everyone left to test their soaring skills at High-Flying Trampoline Dodgeball. "I'm excited to share the court with you," Ellie told Mona and Leona. "No doubt we'll make a mighty team!"

They bounded into the rec center. Campers were hurrying onto the trampoline court. The girls dashed up the stairs to the platform.

"Hold on!" Wendy said, hopping over to them. "One of the dodgeball teams is already full, and the other has only two open spots. One of you will need to sit out."

Ellie turned to the girls while Wendy went to pass out balls. "I can wait for the next game," she said. "Go ahead. You two play together."

"No way!" Leona protested. "Mona got to play with you by herself. Now it's my turn."

Ellie paused. "I suppose that's fair," she replied. "How does that sound to you, Mona?"

Mona's eyes lowered to the ground. "Fine," she said with a shrug. "But Leona can't hog you all day." She glided to the bench and plopped down. A misty cloud puffed out from under her, freezing the bench instantly.

This time Mona is mad at Leona, Ellie thought. *I should try to smooth things over.* She turned toward Mona to do just that, but Leona grabbed her arm.

"C'mon, Ellie!" Leona said, pulling her onto the court. "We'll beat the other team for sure!"

"I can't win," Ellie muttered to herself.

CHAPTER 7

Unfriendly Competition

After dodgeball, the girls raced ahead to the Boom! Pow! Obstacle Course. Ellie fell back to check the description in her camper's guide. It read:

Campers go through a series of superhero-themed obstacles. Only one camper is allowed on the course at a time.

"Only one camper? Phew!" Ellie said with relief. "I'm glad it's not a partner activity. If I had to pick Mona over Leona—or the other way around—one of them would *not* be happy." She clapped the guide closed. "Grumpy heroes are the worst!"

With a burst of super speed, Ellie took off. She caught up with the twins on the field behind the rec center. Her eyes popped at the sight of the obstacle course in the middle of the grassy area. It reminded her of a comic book city!

There were colorful cardboard buildings with paper super-villains peeking out from behind. Each villain had a catch-me-if-you-can look. They were set up around obstacles such as a cargo net and a curvy tunnel.

Wendy was lining up campers. At the head of the line, Mona and Leona waved.

"Ellie, you're going—"

"—first!"

Ellie landed in front of them. "First? Thanks for saving me a spot!"

"Actually," Mona said, "I got here before Leona, so *I* saved the spot for you."

Leona spun toward her sister. "Did not! *I* saved it for Ellie."

They started to argue. Ellie held up her hands, and they settled down. "It was nice of you *both*," she said. "Besides, it's the thought that counts."

Just then, Wendy lifted her clipboard. "All right, everyone!" she said, addressing the crowd. "On my whistle, the first camper will attempt the obstacle course. When that camper has finished, I'll send the next person along." She turned to Ellie. "Ellie, you'll start. Are you ready?"

Feeling unsure, Ellie took her mark. Mona and Leona's behavior bothered her. They weren't being very kind to each other.

It's probably a side effect of the Ultra Hypno Change-O, she figured. She just hoped it would go away before the Super Friend Campfire. The activity was supposed to be for *friends,* but the twins were acting more like enemies.

At Wendy's whistle, Ellie zoomed onto the course. She weaved around cones and crawled through tunnels. "Out of my way, cardboard creeps!" she shouted as super-villains blurred past.

After reaching the top of the cargo net, Ellie jumped down into a foam pit. She rocketed back out and spotted the last obstacle ahead. It was a long balance beam. Bags swung across, ready to knock someone off. Each bag had a sinister-looking face painted on it.

Those no-good bags can't stop me! Ellie thought. Her brainpower fired up, and she started calculating the precise moment to pass through unscathed.

Just then the twins appeared. "Ellie! I saw that you stopped," Mona said, gliding up to Ellie's right side. "Need a hand with this obstacle?"

"I can help!" Leona replied on Ellie's left.

"Uh . . . no, I'm good," Ellie said. "I'm figuring out the best time to cross the beam. I almost have it down to the nanosecond."

But the girls weren't listening. With rocket-force, frost shot from their hands. It hit the bags, freezing them in mid-swing.

The beam was now clear. "Go ahead, Ellie," Leona said proudly. "If you need anything else, give me a shout. That's what friends are for!"

Mona's forehead wrinkled. "*I'm* Ellie's friend," she told Leona. She linked Ellie's arm. "We go together like jingle bells on a sleigh."

Leona took hold of Ellie's other arm. "Well, *we* go together like a pair of skis."

"Like snowcaps on a mountain."

"Like polar bears in the North Pole!"

The girls pulled at Ellie. She felt like she was in the middle of a tug-of-war.

Luckily Wendy came to the rescue. "Oh my!" she said, jogging over. She stared at the bags, which now dripped like melting icicles in the sun. "It appears we have a problem. What happened?"

Mona and Leona let go of Ellie's arms. They turned their backs to one another without saying anything.

"We've had a misunderstanding," Ellie said, speaking for everyone. "But we'll sort it out. It'll be as easy as catching an evildoer."

Wendy offered a cheerful thumbs-up. "I'm glad to hear that," she said. "In the meantime, one camper is allowed on the course. Mona? Leona? You can wait for Ellie back in line."

The girls stayed silent as they left with Wendy. Ellie could tell they were still fighting with each other. It seemed like they were competing to be her friend—in an unfriendly way.

* * *

Over the next two days, the competition continued. On Wednesday Leona snagged the last paddleboat for her and Ellie. They pedaled around the lake, quacking like ducks and making fish faces. When they got back to shore, Mona invited Ellie to make snow angels in the sand—without Leona.

On Thursday the girls tried pulling Ellie onto different sides of the dodgeball court. Ellie's arms hurt as they tugged at her. She wished she could stretch like her Rubberband Dude action figure.

"How about this?" she said, squirming free. "I'll play the first half of the game with one of you.

Then, for the second half, I'll join the other. Fair and square, right?"

To pick who she started with, Ellie eeny, meeny, miny, mo-ed between them. Leona won the first round. While Ellie flew to her side, Leona put her thumb on her nose and wiggled her fingers at Mona. Mona frowned at her sister.

Maybe I should reverse the gadget's effect, Ellie thought. *But what if they leave me out again? The campfire is tomorrow. I don't want to eat s'mores by myself. . . .*

Ignoring the double trouble seemed easiest. Still she couldn't help but notice another effect of the Ultra Hypno Change-O. Mona and Leona were talking separately more than ever. They had always spoken together—that was, before being hypnotized.

It made her worry about the gadget's power. Could it push the twins further apart?

CHAPTER 8

Word War

On Friday, a flurry of chatter filled the campground. Everyone was excited about the campfire festivities. There was talk of sing-alongs, games like Telephone and I Spy, and s'mores on a stick.

But Ellie only heard:

"Sit on *my* raft!"

"Be *my* teammate!"

"Ride bikes with *me*!"

"Go hiking with *me*!"

Mona and Leona fought over Ellie all afternoon. They pulled her in opposite directions, each trying to stop her from playing with the other. Ellie went this way for hopscotch with Mona. She went that way to build sandcastles with Leona. They pulled her around so much that her head started to spin. By nightfall it was moving at warp speed.

Ellie sat dizzily in the arts and crafts hall. It was time for Make-A-Cape, the final activity before the campfire started. On either side of her, the twins decorated plain capes that Wendy had placed on the table.

Mona picked up the tube of silver glitter glue in front of Ellie. "Are you using this, Ellie?" she asked. "I'm going to draw a sparkly snowflake in the center."

"No, go ahead," Ellie replied. She wasn't up to participating. Besides, she didn't need to make a new cape. Hers worked fine already.

"How do you like my drawing, Ellie?" Leona asked. Her cape had a picture of an arctic fox with a purple scarf. "The scarf is the same color as the lightning bolt on your shirt. That bolt is the coolest—just like you!"

Ellie smiled. "Thanks, Leona," she replied. "You know, you're a super friend."

Overhearing that, Mona turned in her seat. She looked troubled. "Wait," she said to Ellie. "I thought *I* was your super friend."

"Oh sure," Ellie added quickly. She worried she had said something wrong. "You are too, Mona."

"Of course, I'm *more* super," Leona said. She scooted her chair closer to Ellie's. "I hung out with Ellie this week while *someone* tagged along like a sidekick. I won't say the person's name. But it starts with an *M* and ends with an *ona*."

"A sidekick?" Mona bristled at her sister. "If you look up that word in the dictionary, you'll see your freckle-faced picture." She held her chin high. "I'm Ellie's real friend. Not you."

"Nuh-uh!"

"Yuh-huh!"

The girls went back and forth. Ellie listened to their voices clash until her stomach turned. She couldn't take their arguing anymore.

"I'm not feeling very well," she said, interrupting. "I'd better go back to the cabin."

Leaving Mona and Leona behind, Ellie flew into the night. *What was I thinking using the Ultra Hypno Change-O on them?* she scolded herself.

Sure it had made the twins treat Ellie better. But it had also had the *opposite* effect on the way they treated each other. It had turned them into archenemies instead of best friends.

Mom was right, Ellie thought. *Sometimes power can do more harm than good.*

Hopefully being back in the cabin alone would give her time to clear her mind. The girls' friendship needed to be fixed, and only she had the power to do that. Just then an envelope on her bed caught her eye. It was pink with a picture of a dancing ballerina.

Ellie's heart leaped. "Hannah wrote back!" She raced to the envelope and pulled out the letter. It read:

Hi Ellie!

I miss YOU! This week has been B–O–R–I–N–G. Being on little-sister patrol stinks! Thanks to Cece, I've had to watch every episode of "Boogie-Woogie Woodchuck."

(Yesterday I started singing the theme song. It's taking over my brain!)

I'm sorry your cabinmates are being mean. They shouldn't treat a fellow hero like that. Maybe you can ask them why? If you knew the reason, it might help you get to know them better. Good luck!

YSB,

Hannah

P.S. Save me from the "Boogie-Woogie Woodchuck." PLEASE.

As Ellie put the letter away, she thought hard about Hannah's advice. It made sense to ask the girls why they disliked her. She might not like their answer, but it was part of getting to know them. If they still didn't want to be friends after that, at least she'd have tried.

First I have to make them friends again. But that should be simple, Ellie figured. All she had to do was have them look at the Hypno Change-O again. Then she could reverse the invention's effects.

Ellie ran to her bag and took out the gadget. She was ready to go when the door opened. Mona and Leona skated inside, snow flurries whirling around them.

"Ellie, we've come to a conclusion," Mona said.

"We're done fighting," Leona added.

Ellie's mouth fell open. "Really? What a relief!" she replied. "It's no fun when you aren't getting along."

"I agree," Mona continued as her sister nodded. "So we decided to have you settle our argument. Tell us, who is your more super friend? Me—"

"—or me?" Leona said.

CHAPTER 9

A Super Showdown

Flurries swirled angrily around the cabin. The twins were growing impatient waiting for Ellie to choose which one of them was the more super friend. But how could she pick only one? It would cause even frostier feelings.

Leona glided forward. "I can help you decide, Ellie," she said. "I'll prove my super-ness. Watch!"

She rubbed her hands together, and a sparkling mist sprinkled down from them. A moment later, she opened them, revealing a necklace made of ice crystals. The necklace shined like a diamond.

"Whoa! That's incredible, Leona!" Ellie said.

"Oh, that's nothing," Mona said, waving Leona's handiwork away. She stepped in front of her sister. "I can do way better. Wait until you see this. . . ."

She skated over to the wall and tossed mist on an empty hanger. A shimmering gown took shape. It had a snow-white sash and bow.

"It's a whole dress made of ice," Mona bragged. "Super, huh?"

"Hmmph," Leona grumbled as Ellie admired the frozen frock. She blew ice crystals into her palm, and a miniature ice sculpture of Ellie sprang up. "Here, Ellie! How would you like a statue of yourself?"

"How about a *life-size* statue?" Mona countered. She blew at the ground with the biggest breath she could muster. Ice formed a new Ellie sculpture. It stood eye-to-eye with Ellie, its cape stuck in mid-flight.

With a huff, Leona slid Mona's statue against the wall. She flexed her fingers, then filled the empty space with a lion sculpture. Mona pushed the lion aside, responding with an ice sculpture of the Sphinx.

The twins dueled back and forth, making animals and monuments from around the world. Soon the room was an exhibit of subzero masterpieces.

It's getting downright chilly in here, Ellie thought as the cabin got colder and colder. Her heating power kept her warm enough. But she kicked herself for not packing a sweater.

It was time to stop the showdown. "Leona! Mona!" Ellie ran over to them with the Hypno

Change-O. "I know you want to outdo each other, but it's gone too far. It's hurting your friendship! Look here, OK? I can fix everything!"

Ellie held out the gadget, but the girls paid no attention. Mona was too busy one-upping Leona's self-portrait with a frosty picture of the *Mona Lisa*. Leona pointed at Mona. As her hand flew forward, it collided with the Hypno Change-O, knocking the gadget out of Ellie's grasp. It sailed across the room and landed in the corner.

"I challenge you to a snowman-building contest!" Leona said to her sister. "The first person done is the winner."

Mona's eyes narrowed. "Challenge accepted."

Snow sprayed from the twins' fingertips, covering the floor in a thick blanket. They set to work packing and stacking the flakes until a pair of plump snowmen stood in front of them. Then

they grabbed buttons from some old crafts and stuck on eyes and a mouth. With that finished, they raced outside for pine cone noses.

Taking advantage of the moment, Ellie zoomed across the room to retrieve the gadget. But halfway there her hot heels slipped on a patch of ice.

"Yikes!" she cried. She skidded out of control and crashed into Mona's snowman. The creation toppled into a lopsided lump.

Ellie was picking herself up when Leona returned. Mona skated in soon after and gasped with outrage.

"Leona, you wrecked my snowman!" she cried. "Did you realize you were going to lose?"

"Me? *Lose?*" Leona turned smugly away from her sister. "Face it. I could beat you even in a snowball fight."

"Prove it!"

Mona began to spin around. She twirled faster on one side of the room while Leona started spinning on the other side. They rotated in tornado-like funnels, only the winds that circled them weren't sucking in anything. Instead, snowflakes appeared in the blustery air. The flakes stuck together, little by little, until they collected into powdery balls of snow.

Suddenly . . . *zing! Zing! Zing!* Snowballs flew as the girls launched them at each other. They smashed against the walls, doors, and ceiling. One of the balls struck a sign that read *Rules for the Cabin*. Unfortunately, *No Snowball Fights* wasn't a rule.

Ducking for cover, Ellie picked up the Hypno Change-O. A snowball whooshed overhead and smashed into a photo taped on Mona's cabinet. In the picture, the twins were sharing a sled and giggling.

I need to put a stop to this, Ellie thought. *It's the only way to save their friendship. But how am I going to make them look at the gadget?*

The twins were sure to keep battling, blizzard style, until the cabin turned into an igloo. That was the problem with superheroes—stopping them would take something *extra*ordinary.

CHAPTER 10

A New Beginning

Ideas rushed through Ellie's mind at high speed. She needed a way to break up Mona and Leona's fight, once and for all.

She could try to stop their snowballs. But they were throwing too many. Even if she had a ball-fetching expert like Super Fluffy at her side, it would be impossible to nab them all.

Maybe I could build a wall between them? Ellie wondered. But the snow from their blizzards would still pile up in the cabin. In no time, it would pour out of the windows like an avalanche!

If I needed help, then they would look over, Ellie thought, her brainpower going into overdrive. Nothing grabbed a superhero's attention like someone who had to be rescued. *Wait! That's it!*

Gusty flakes circled the spinning twins. Ellie spun herself in the other direction, making her own cyclone-force wind. The wind worked like a vacuum, pulling in the snowflakes that whipped around the room.

The snow began to surround Ellie. It started out low, gathering at her ankles. Soon it climbed higher and higher as the wind swept in more and more flakes. It buried her waist, then her shoulders. Ellie stopped when it reached her chin. She looked like she was trapped in a giant snow cone.

"Help, I'm stuck!" she shouted, punching her arms out of the powder. Waving frantically, she tried to do her best save-me impression. "I need a superhero! I can't get out of here on my own!"

"Ellie?" The twins twirled to a halt. "Hold on! We're coming!"

Leona hurried over with Mona. Ellie wiggled loose enough to put the Hypno Change-O in reverse. Then she turned the gadget face-out. The lines swirled backward, drawing the twins in. A thick haze fell over their eyes. Seconds later it lifted like a morning fog.

The twins double-blinked.

"What happened—"

"—in here?"

They glanced around the room. Leona stared with wonder at the ice sculptures. Looking perplexed, Mona picked a snowball off the floor.

They didn't seem to remember their battle—or being hypnotized—at all.

Ellie freed herself from the snow. She gave it a super-heated blast, and it evaporated into thin air. "It's a long story," she told them. "I was trying to be your friend, but I went about it the wrong way. I got in the middle of you two and caused a major fight. I didn't mean to, and I'm really sorry."

"We were fighting?" Mona raised a curious eyebrow. "That's weird. We usually get along."

"Mona's right," Leona replied. She turned to her sister. "In fact, when was the last time we disagreed?" She thought for a moment. "Oh yeah! Our birthday. We both wanted to ride our new sled. Since we couldn't decide who went first, we rode at the same time. It was a blast!"

"It sounds like you're very close," Ellie said. She took a deep breath. "I want to talk to you about that, actually. I was hoping to get to know you both, maybe even be friends with you. But when I tried, you ignored me. Why?"

The room got quiet as the girls shared a long look. "We've been kind of cold, huh?" Mona asked.

Ellie nodded. "It made me feel really bad. Worse than letting an evildoer get away, even."

"We weren't trying to be mean," Leona said, stepping forward. "We just like doing things together. Mona and I are best friends."

"We weren't sure someone else would fit into our friendship," Mona added. "But it wasn't nice to leave you out. We should've given you a chance." She gave Ellie a warm look. "Maybe we can start over? If only we had the power to go back in time. . . ."

We could all go to the past, Ellie thought. They would only need the Ultra Time Traveler. But it was probably best not to use the gadget. If she turned the dial too much, they could wind up in the Stone Age.

"We're sorry," the girls said. "Will you forgive us?"

Ellie was about to answer when she heard someone knocking. The door opened, and Wendy walked into the room.

"Snazzy statue!" Wendy said, spotting the life-size sculpture of Ellie. She marveled at the hero on ice, then turned to everyone. "The campfire is starting. You super friends are coming, right?"

Ellie smiled at the twins. "We'll be there," she answered.

"Great! You'll hear me play my harmonica," Wendy replied. "People say I'm a whiz at the instrument—that's how I got my superhero name!"

As the counselor left, a new idea struck Ellie. "I think we really can start over," she told the girls. "Let's pretend like we're meeting for the first time." She straightened up and stood tall. "Hi, I'm Ellie! Do you want to do the hero handshake?"

"Sure!" the twins replied.

The three of them fist-bumped. Then they swung at the air. After that, their hands went on their hips as their shoulders flew back.

Winning grins spread across their faces. "You know—" Mona began.

"—we strike this pose—" Leona continued.

"—whenever we stop—"

"—a super-villain."

"It's funny," Ellie replied with a giggle. "I was thinking the same thing!"

CHAPTER 11

S'mores and Smiles

The Super Friend Campfire cast an inviting glow over the clearing. All around, campers sat and talked. Wendy and the other counselors stood nearby, giving out s'mores on sticks.

Ellie licked her lips at the platter that Wendy was holding. It was piled with long lollipop sticks, each topped with toasted marshmallows. The treats had been dipped in gooey chocolate and crumbled graham crackers.

"Three, please!" Ellie said.

"Wow! Heroes sure have mighty appetites," Wendy replied. She leaned in closer and winked. "Just kidding! The treats are for you and your friends, right?"

Ellie laughed. "You read my mind."

"We're right here, Ellie!" Mona called, waving from her spot on a log bench. She scooted over, and Leona patted the space between them.

"We saved a seat—"

"—for you!"

With a smile, Ellie joined the girls. She was happy the twins were friends again. But she was equally glad to have their friendship. It was better than anything she could create with a do-gooding gadget.

"Here you go," she said, handing over the tasty treats. "If the s'mores are cold, just let me know.

I can warm them up with my heating power. No campfire needed!"

"Actually, we love cold treats," they replied.

"Frozen yogurt, ice cream bars, fruit pops—"

"—you name it!"

Ellie and the twins celebrated the night in true super-friend style. They giggled together during a silly sing-along. Then they clapped and whistled as Wendy played her harmonica. She was a real music-making whiz!

Next they played I Spy. Mona spied a star that sparkled like a snowflake, and Leona saw a constellation that was shaped like an iceberg. Ellie spotted something gold with a picture of ice skates.

"It's my figure skating medal!" Mona said, pointing to the award dangling around her neck. She turned to Ellie. "You know, you should try ice skating again. Maybe Leona and I can give you lessons?"

"I could use the practice," Ellie replied. "But I have a favor to ask . . . could you make the ice a bit softer?"

Just then Wendy stood up on a bench. "Heroes, we have one last activity!" she announced. "We're going to play Telephone. The rules are simple: one camper will whisper a phrase to the camper next to her or him. Then we'll share the phrase around the circle. Let's see if it stays the same!" She pointed at Mona. "Mona? Go ahead and get us started. Maybe you can share your favorite book character?"

Mona nodded, then whispered something to the boy next to her. Ellie covered her ears so she couldn't listen in supersonically. She was the last camper in the circle and didn't want to cheat.

The phrase went from one person to another. It finally came all the way around. Leona leaned over and whispered in Ellie's ear.

Ellie's eyes widened in surprise. "Is it . . . Princess Power?" she asked.

"That's right!" the twins said. "We have all the comic books."

"They have good ideas—"

"—for busting bad guys."

"So true!" Ellie exclaimed. "I used *The Staff and the Spell* to stop a royally wicked bug. It tried to take over my school spelling bee, but I taught that villain a lesson."

"We'll close the night with our official cheer," Wendy said. "Ready? One . . . two . . . three . . ."

"Let's hear it for the camp," everyone sang, "where the action never ends!"

"Camp Hero—" said Mona.

"—Camp Hero—" Leona added.

Beaming, Ellie finished, "—the place for super friends!"

* * *

Everyone spent the next morning packing up after breakfast. Camp had come to an end.

Ellie tucked the final few comic books into her suitcase. The twins took great interest in Ice Boy, so she let them keep one of the comics. She already had plenty of books from the collection at home.

As she zipped her bag, Mona pointed to the Ultra Hypno Change-O on Ellie's bed. "Hey, don't forget your invention thingy," she said. "It's so neat! Can we see how it works?"

Ellie shivered just thinking about the mess it had made. "Um . . . I'd better not," she replied, slipping the gadget into her pocket. "It's really powerful. Power like that can cause twice the trouble."

Suddenly Wendy popped into the doorway. "Hey, Kid Wonders! It's time to head out," she said. "I can carry some luggage if anyone needs help."

"We're OK, thanks!" the twins replied. An ice path formed under them, and they slid their bags out of the cabin.

Flexing her muscle power, Ellie scooped up her suitcase. Then she and the twins followed Wendy to the parking lot. Some very special people were waiting!

"Mom! Dad!" Ellie shouted. She ran over and gave them the tightest hug ever.

"Whew! I'm happy to see you too, my hero," Mom said, catching her breath. "How was your week?"

"Did you have a nice break from doing chores and battling slime?" Dad asked.

Ellie was about to answer her parents when the girls came over with an older man. He had a frosty wisp of hair on his head.

"Grandpa, this is Ellie," Mona told him.

Leona patted Ellie's shoulder. "She's our good friend."

"It's nice to meet you, Ellie," the girls' grandpa said. He waved, and a few snowflakes flew off his hand.

"Can we please come back to camp next year?" the twins asked him.

"We can't wait to—"

"—see Ellie again!"

"Maybe I can bring along my best friend, Hannah," Ellie said. "She doesn't stop getaway

GLOSSARY

conclusion (kuhn-KLOO-zhuhn)—a final decision reached by reasoning

clone (klohn)—to make an exact copy of something

cooperative (koh-OP-er-uh-tiv)—willing to go along with or work with others

craft (kraft)—a boat, especially one of small size

festivities (fes-TIV-i-tees)—joyful, fun activities

handiwork (HAN-dee-wurk)—work done personally

impatient (im-PAY-shuhnt)—restless and eager

minion (MIN-yuhn)—a person who obediently serves or works for a usually powerful person or organization

quarters (KWOR-turs)—living accomodations

stationery (STAY-shuh-ner-ee)—materials, such as paper, pens, and ink, for writing or typing

sullen (SUHL-uhn)—gloomily or resentfully silent

TALK ABOUT ELLIE!

1. Ellie feels excluded by Mona and Leona when she first arrives at Camp Hero. Talk about a time a friend, classmate, or fellow camper made you feel left out. How did you handle the situation?

2. Super friends play together and try to give each other good advice. They also have stuff in common—Ellie and the twins all love Princess Power! Talk about what else makes a friend super.

3. Ellie finds herself in the middle of Mona and Leona's argument. Pretend two of your friends are not getting along. Talk about how you can help solve their conflict.

EXPRESS YOURSELF!

1. Hannah teaches Ellie the special camp greeting before she leaves. Make up your own hero handshake. When you're done, teach it to a friend or sibling.

2. Ellie hopes to have fun with Mona and Leona. As superheroes, they can save a town or two! Take the trio on a mighty adventure and write a story about them.

3. One camp activity is the Boom! Pow! Obstacle Course. It has exciting obstacles, such as a cargo net and foam pit. On a sheet of paper, draw your own obstacle course for Camp Hero.

ABOUT THE AUTHOR

Gina Bellisario is an ordinary grown-up who can do many extraordinary things. She can make things disappear, such as a cheeseburger or a grass stain. She can create a masterpiece out of glitter glue and shoelaces. She can even thwart a messy room with her super cleaning power! Gina lives in Park Ridge, Illinois, not too far from Winkopolis, with her husband and their super kids.

ABOUT THE ILLUSTRATOR

Jessika von Innerebner loves creating—especially when it inspires and empowers others to make the world a better place. She landed her first illustration job at the age of seventeen and hasn't looked back since. Jess is an illustrator who loves humor and heart and has colored her way through projects with Disney.com, Nickelodeon, Fisher-Price, and Atomic Cartoons, to name a few. In her spare moments, Jess can be found long-boarding, yoga-ing, dancing, adventuring to distant lands, and laughing with friends. She currently lives in sunny Kelowna, Canada.

ONLY FROM CAPSTONE!

THE FUN DOESN'T STOP HERE!

Discover more at *www.capstonekids.com*

Videos and Contests
Games and Puzzles
Friends and Favorites
Authors and Illustrators

Find cool websites and more books like this one
at *www.facthound.com.* Just type in the
Book ID: 9781496565136 and you're ready to go!